IN HIS STEPS

Charles M. Sheldon

Retold by Dan Larsen

Illustrated by Kevin Owen

BARBOUR
PUBLISHING, INC.
Uhrichsville, Ohio

© MCMXC by Barbour Publishing, Inc.

ISBN 1-55748-137-7

All Scripture quotations are taken from the Authorized King James Version of the Bible.

Published by Barbour Publishing, Inc.
        P.O. Box 719
        Uhrichsville, Ohio 44683
        http://www.barbourbooks.com

Member of the
Evangelical Christian
Publishers Association

Printed in the United States of America.

IN HIS STEPS

Contents

Looks like a tramp

1
A Stranger

The Rev. Henry Maxwell had just sat down at his desk when the doorbell rang. *Now what!* he thought. He was growing nervous. It was Friday morning, and he was trying to finish his Sunday sermon. He had already been interrupted several times this morning, and his sermon was going very slowly.

Frowning, he looked out his window to the sidewalk below. *Looks like a tramp,* he said to himself. He went downstairs and opened the door.

On the step outside was a young man dressed in shabby clothes. He was pale and unshaven. He clutched a hat with both hands. The two men stood looking at each other for a moment without speaking. Then the young man cleared his throat and said, "I'm out of a job, sir, and thought maybe you might put me in the way of finding something."

"I don't know of anything," said Henry. "Jobs are scarce." He started to shut the door. Before he could, the man spoke again.

"I didn't know if you might be able to give me a line to the city railway or the superintendent of the shops, or something," he said, shifting his hat nervously from hand to hand.

"It would be of no use," said Henry quickly. "You must excuse me. I'm very busy this morning. I hope you find something." This time he did shut the door.

Back upstairs, he looked out his window again. He watched the man walk down the front steps and turn onto the street. He went very slowly, his shoulders sagging.

He went very slowly

A STRANGER

Henry stared at the figure for a moment. Then he shook his head and sat down again to work. The text he was using for his sermon was from 1 Peter 2:21. "It was to this that God called you, for Christ himself suffered for you and left you an example, so that you would follow in his steps."

He wrote quickly now. He wanted his sermon to cover Christ's example for people, how he suffered for us, and how he became a sacrifice for us by giving up his life for us. "We are to follow Christ's example," Henry wrote, "by living our lives the way he lived his."

* * *

"A queer thing happened at the kindergarten this morning," Henry's wife, Mary, said as they

"We are to follow Christ's example"

ate dinner that night. "I was visiting the school today, you remember. Well, as the children were all at their desks, a young man came in and sat down. He was some kind of tramp by the look of him, holding a dirty hat in both hands. Miss Wren and her assistant, Miss Kyle, were a little frightened at first, but he sat there very quietly and after a few minutes went out."

Henry stopped chewing. "Did you say he looked like a tramp?" he asked.

"Yes, very dusty and shabby looking. Not much more than thirty, I'd say."

"The same man came here, I think," he said, rubbing his chin slowly. He was silent for a while.

Then Mary changed the subject, and they began talking about other things.

Sunday morning came bright and clear to the town of Raymond. At eleven o'clock the First

"Did you say he looked like a tramp?"

A STRANGER

Church of Raymond was filled with the town's best-dressed, best-known people. The congregation seemed to wax and wane with the changing of the weather. Today was clear and warm, and the pews were full. Henry had worked especially hard on his sermon for today, and now he was quietly excited that so many had come to hear it.

The First Church had the best of everything. The walls were covered with ornately carved oak paneling. The stained-glass windows were rich and glowing. Even the choir, a professional quartet, was the best that money could buy.

The soprano was a young woman named Rachel Winslow. She was very beautiful, with dark eyes, jet-black hair, and an olive complexion. This morning all eyes were on her as she stood up to sing a solo.

"Where he leads me I will follow.
I'll go with him all the way."

Today was clear and warm

Her face was radiant. *Her voice had never sounded so beautiful,* Henry thought with pride. When she sat down a murmur ran through the congregation, as if the people had all they could do to keep from clapping and cheering.

Henry's sermon that morning was just as stirring. His manner was polished, and his tone was eloquent. He didn't chide in his preaching, or speak harsh words to turn sinners to God. He spoke encouraging, soothing words, and his listeners' faces showed their contentment with his sermon. He spoke of following Christ's example. When he was through, the quartet sang a final hymn.

> "All for Jesus, all for Jesus.
> All my being's ransomed powers . . ."

Henry's heart was soaring. *A perfect finale*

Her voice had never sounded so beautiful.

for a perfect service, he thought.

Just then something happened. It wasn't what anyone expected, not what anyone had come to see or hear. But it would change the First Church of Raymond forever.

A quiet voice came from the rear of the church.

"I've been wondering since I came in here if it would be just the thing to say a word at the close of the service," said a man now standing in the aisle.

Everyone had turned and was staring at him. He was shabby looking, holding his hat in front of him. Henry stared the hardest of anyone. It was the tramp, the man who had come to his door just a couple of days ago. But now he seemed even paler, even thinner. His face looked even sadder.

The man began slowly walking toward the

A quiet voice came from the rear of the church.

front. "I'm not drunk," he said, slowly, quietly. "And I'm not crazy. I'm perfectly harmless. But if I die, as I probably will in a few days, I want the satisfaction of thinking that I had my say in a place like this, and before this sort of crowd."

As the man spoke, Henry's face grew white and grave. No one moved or spoke as the man continued, standing now in front, facing the congregation.

"I'm not an ordinary tramp, though I don't know of any teaching of Jesus that makes one kind of a tramp less worth saving than another. Do you?"

The question wasn't challenging or mocking. It was just a question, and it came out very mildly and unthreateningly. He coughed and doubled over in pain. Then he went on.

"I lost my job ten months ago. I am a printer by trade. The new linotype machines are

I'm not crazy.

beautiful inventions, but I know six men who have killed themselves this year just because of those machines. Of course I don't blame the newspapers for getting the machines, but meanwhile what can a man do? That's the only trade I know. I've tramped all over the country trying to find something. There are a lot of others like me. I'm not complaining, just stating facts.

"But I was wondering," he continued, "as I sat there in back, if what you call following Jesus is the same thing as what he taught. What did he mean when he said to follow him? The minister here today said that disciples of Jesus must follow in his steps, the steps of obedience, faith, love, and imitation. But I didn't hear him say what that really means, especially imitation. What do you Christians mean by following the steps of Jesus?

"I've tramped through this city for three days

What do you Christians mean by following the steps of Jesus?

trying to find a job. In all that time no one except your minister here has had one word of sympathy. I suppose you get so used to the professional tramps that you've lost interest in any other sort.''

He stopped and held up a hand, as if to ask for pardon. His voice was mild, even painful, but not accusing.

''I know you can't go out of your way to hunt up a job for someone like me,'' he continued. ''And I'm not asking you to. But I'm puzzled. What do you mean when you sing 'I'll go with him, with him, all the way'? Do you mean that you are suffering and denying yourselves and trying to save lost people, the way Jesus did?''

He stopped again, as if to catch his breath. He was weaving slightly now, and had to lean a hand on the front rail. And now his eyes were full of pain.

''My wife died four months ago,'' he said slowly.

"My wife died four months ago."

A STRANGER

"I'm glad she is out of trouble. My little girl is staying with a printer's family until I find a job. Somehow I get puzzled when I see so many Christians living in luxury, singing about following Jesus, and then remember my wife dying in a New York tenement house, gasping for air and asking God to take the little girl too. The owner of that tenement house was a member of a church, and I understand a lot of tenement owners are Christians. I wonder if following Christ is true in their case. I heard some people singing at a church prayer meeting the other night. 'All for Jesus, all for Jesus, all my being's ransomed powers. All my thoughts, and all my doings, all my days and all my hours.' I kept wondering as I sat on the steps outside what they meant by it. I wonder if a lot of trouble in the world wouldn't exist if all the people who sing such songs went and lived them out.

All my being's ransomed powers.

"It seems to me sometimes as if the people in the big churches have nice houses and money for luxuries and go away on summer vacations, while the people outside the churches die in tenements, walk the streets for jobs, never have a piano or a picture in the house, and grow up in misery and drunkenness and sin."

Suddenly he lurched forward and fell in the middle of the aisle. He lay facedown, his hat clutched in one hand.

He lay facedown, his hat clutched in one hand.

"Our brother passed away this morning."

2
Henry Maxwell

It was a week later, Sunday morning. Henry Maxwell stood before a full congregation. But today something was very wrong. Henry didn't speak forcefully, or even clearly. Though his mouth spoke the words, sometimes almost mumbling, his mind seemed somewhere else. He looked tired, even smaller somehow.

When his sermon was finished, he shut his Bible and stepped out from the pulpit. "Our brother passed away this morning," he said slowly.

People looked at one another. Everyone knew Henry meant the strange young man who had spoken last Sunday and collapsed in the aisle. The talk had gone all over town. The man had been brought to Henry's house and had lain there all week, unconscious. No one but Henry knew that very early this morning the man had come to just long enough to ask about his little daughter and to thank Henry for his kindness. Then he had turned his head slowly to one side and died quietly.

Henry had stayed up almost every night, sitting at the man's side. The strain was showing in his face now. "The things this stranger said last week have made a very powerful impression on me," he said. "All week long, and especially with this man's death in my house, I have been bothered by the question of what Jesus would do. I can't really say that any of us have not acted like Christ toward this man, or toward others like him in the world. But I believe that what he said was so vitally true that we must face the question of what it means to follow in

Sitting at the man's side.

Christ's steps, or else be condemned as Christian disciples."

All eyes were on Henry. No one moved or made a sound.

"What I am about to propose now should not seem unusual or impossible," said Henry. "I would like volunteers from the First Church to commit themselves for an entire year to not do anything without first asking what Jesus would do. After asking that question, each one will follow Jesus exactly as he taught his disciples to do, no matter what the result may be. I will, of course, include myself in this company of volunteers. At the close of the service I would like everyone who wishes to make this commitment to meet in the lecture room, and we will discuss further what this means."

After Henry dismissed the service, a murmur rose among the people as they moved toward the

All eyes were on Henry.

exits, everyone talking about this strange new idea. Henry stayed for a few minutes at the door, greeting people as they left. When the church had emptied, he went to the lecture room.

As he opened the door he stopped in midstep and stared. He had no idea that so many people would accept his challenge. About fifty people were waiting for him. There was Edward Norman, editor of the Raymond newspaper, the *Daily News*. Alexander Powers, superintendent of the great railroad shops. Donald Marsh, president of Lincoln College. Milton Wright, one of the great merchants of Raymond. Dr. West, considered an authority in surgery. Jasper Chase, an author who had written one successful novel and was said to be working on another. Miss Virginia Page, who had recently inherited a fortune with her brother. And Rachel Winslow, the young soprano and good friend of Virginia's. There

About fifty people were waiting for him.

were many others too.

"Let's first ask for God's guidance," Henry said, bowing his head to pray. When he looked up, his face was wet with tears. Now his voice trembled slightly as he spoke. "We all understand what we have agreed to do," he said. "We pledge ourselves to do nothing in our daily lives without first asking what Jesus would do. Regardless of what the result may be to us. Sometime I will be able to tell you of the marvelous change that has come over my life this week, but not now. Since what happened last Sunday, I have become uneasy over my ideas of following Christ. And this is why I have decided to do this. I didn't dare do it alone. I know I am being guided by the hand of divine love in this. That same divine love must have led all of you, too. Now, do we all understand what we are to do?"

His face was wet with tears.

"I want to ask a question," said Rachel Winslow. "I am not quite sure how to know what Jesus would do. We live in such a different age now. There are many things in life now that aren't mentioned in the teachings of Jesus. How am I going to tell what he would do?"

"We must study Jesus by the power of his spirit," said Henry. "You remember what he said to his disciples." He opened his Bible and read John 16:13-15: 'When the spirit comes, who reveals the truth about God, he will lead you into all the truth. He will not speak on his own authority, but he will speak of what he hears and will tell you of things to come. He will give me glory, because he will take what I say and tell it to you. All that my Father has is mine; that is why I said that the spirit will take what I give him and tell it to you.'

"There is no other test that I know of,"

He opened his Bible and read
John 16:13-15

continued Henry. "To decide what Jesus would do, we will have to go to that source of knowledge."

"What if others say that what we're doing is not what Jesus would do?" asked Alexander Powers.

"We can't help that," said Henry. "But we must be absolutely honest with ourselves. Our standard of Christian action cannot vary from act to act."

"But what one person thinks Jesus would do may not be the same as what another thinks," said Donald Marsh. "Will it be possible to reach the same conclusions in all cases?"

Henry didn't answer for a while. Finally he said, "When it comes to a genuine, honest following in Jesus' steps, I cannot believe there will be any confusion about the truth of our judgments. We must first find out what Jesus

"What if others say that what we're doing is not what Jesus would do?"

said in the Word, and then ask for guidance from his spirit.

"But we must remember this great fact," continued Henry. "After we have asked the spirit to tell us what Jesus would do, and have received an answer, we are to act, no matter what happens to us. Is that understood?"

He looked around the room at all the silent faces. Everyone met his gaze squarely, and everyone nodded solemnly.

They all agreed to meet every week to share their experiences with one another. Then, one by one, everyone left.

When Henry got home he went into his study, where the man's body lay. He stood there looking at that white face, the eyes closed forever. And in Henry's heart he cried out, *Lord, help me! Give me strength and wisdom to follow you!*

Lord, help me! Give me strength and wisdom to follow you!

"Here's the press report of yesterday's fight."

3
Ed Norman

Clark looked excited as he rushed into Ed Norman's office carrying some typewritten sheets. "Here's the press report of yesterday's prize fight," he said.

It was Monday morning. Ed had gone into his office at the *Daily News* early. He had sat at his desk and done some very hard thinking. Yesterday in the lecture room at church it had seemed almost easy to make the commitment to follow Jesus in everything. But this morning, facing another busy week at the newspaper, he wasn't so sure.

He laid the sheets out on his desk. Clark stood grinning. "It'll make three and a half columns," Clark said. "It all goes in, right?" He turned to leave.

"No," said Ed. "We won't run this today."

Clark stopped as if he had been struck from behind. "What?"

"Leave it out of the paper," said Ed. "We won't use it."

Clark didn't speak for a moment. He stood staring at Ed. Clark was the managing editor at the paper, next to Ed Norman in authority. Ed liked to know everything that happened in the newspaper offices, so Clark brought everything to Ed for approval, even though Clark knew Ed would always approve whatever he brought him.

Now Clark couldn't believe what he had just heard. He walked slowly back into Ed's office. "But —"

"Clark, I don't think it ought to be printed."

"Do you mean that the paper is going to press without a word of the prize fight in it?"

We won't run this today

"Yes, that's what I mean."

"But it's unheard of! All the other papers will print it. What will our readers say?"

"Come in here a minute, Clark," Ed said quietly. "And shut the door."

Clark sat down. The two men stared at each other for a minute. Then Ed said, "Clark, if Jesus Christ were editor of a newspaper, do you honestly think he would print three and a half columns about a bloody prize fight?"

"No, I don't suppose he would," said Clark.

"Well, that's my only reason for shutting this account out of the *News*. I have decided not to do anything that I honestly believe Jesus wouldn't do."

Clark couldn't speak for a minute. When he finally found his voice, he said, "What effect will it have on the paper?"

"What do you think?" asked Ed.

"What do you think?"

"I think it will ruin the paper! You just can't run a paper nowadays on such a basis. It's too ideal. The world isn't ready for it. You can't make it pay. Just as sure as you live, if you shut out this prize fight, you'll lose hundreds of customers. The very best people in town are eager to read it. They know the fight happened yesterday, and when they get the paper tonight, they'll expect half a page at least. You can't afford to ignore the wishes of the public. It'll be a great mistake if you do, in my opinion."

Ed was silent for a while, thinking. Then he said, "Clark, in your honest opinion, what is the right standard for our behavior? Isn't the only right standard for everyone the standard of Jesus? Wouldn't you say that the best law for people to live by is found in asking what Jesus would do, and then following it as closely as possible?"

Clark's face reddened a bit, and he twisted in

What is the right standard for
our behavior?

his chair. "Well . . . yes . . . I suppose if you talk of what people should do, then, yes, there is no other standard of behavior. But the question is, is it possible to make it pay? To succeed in the newspaper business, we've got to do what the world expects. We can't act as if we were living in an ideal world."

"Do you mean that we can't run this paper strictly on Christian principles and make it succeed?"

Clark stood up quickly. "Yes! That's exactly what I mean. It can't be done. We'll go broke in a month."

"We'll have to talk about this further, Clark. But meanwhile, we need to understand each other. I've promised not to do anything for a whole year without asking myself what Jesus would do in my place. And I believe that by doing this we'll not only succeed, but succeed better

We'll go broke in a month.

than we ever did.''

"The report doesn't go in?" asked Clark, staring hard.

"No. We have plenty of good stuff to take its place. We'll act as if there were no such thing as a prize fight yesterday.''

Before noon that day, everyone at the newspaper had heard that the prize fight story wouldn't be in the paper. Whenever Ed walked through an office he would hear everything grow quiet and would feel the stares. He knew everyone must be talking about him, wondering if he had lost his mind.

Maybe it would be a lonely journey, but he was determined to follow Jesus in everything.

That night on his way home, Ed came down the stairs into the main office. The room was full of paperboys, all shouting at George, the desk clerk. Bundles of newspapers lay strewn all over

The room was full of paperboys.

the floor.

"What's the matter, George?" asked Ed.

"The boys can't sell any of their papers because the fight isn't in it," said George, eyeing Ed sharply.

Ed thought for a minute. Then he walked up to the boys. "Boys, count out your papers, and I'll buy them myself."

Suddenly everything was quiet. The boys stared at one another for a moment, then all rushed to their bundles and began counting loudly and furiously.

"Give them their money, George," Ed said over the noise. "And if any others come in, buy their papers, too." He turned to the boys. "Is that fair, boys?"

"Fair!" one said, his mouth open. "I'll say! But how long are you gonna keep this up?"

Ed just smiled and went out. On the walk

*"Boys, count out your papers,
and I'll buy them myself."*

home he wondered if what he had done was what Jesus would do. *After all,* he thought, *it wasn't the boys' fault they couldn't sell the papers.* No one else should have to suffer from his decision, he told himself. He would pay the price himself, take the blame himself. He had suspected that sales would drop because of his decisions, so this didn't come as a big surprise. Still . . .

That week the mail started pouring in. Customer after customer cancelled their subscriptions because of no fight story in Monday's *News.* Ed had been expecting this.

But then one letter came from a large tobacco dealer in the city, cancelling its advertising with the paper. This company had done business for years with the *News,* paying a very good price for its advertising space.

On reading this letter, Ed sat thinking for a while. He hadn't given any thought to the

*That week the mail started
pouring in.*

advertisements in the paper. As he looked over the columns he saw several ads that he didn't believe Jesus would print if he were editor. Many of them were for liquor and tobacco. Liquor was a big business in Raymond, maybe the biggest. Saloons and pool halls were everywhere. It was all legitimate, licensed business, Ed knew. And they all advertised with the paper. What would the paper do if he cut out all that advertising? Could it survive? That was the question.

No, that was not the question. The question, he knew, was what would Jesus do? Would Jesus advertise whiskey in his paper?

Ed sighed deeply and called Clark into his office. "Clark, I've decided to cut some of these ads as soon as their contracts run out. Would you please tell the advertising agent not to renew the ads I've circled here?"

Clark looked grim as he glanced over the

I've decided to cut some of these ads.

columns of ads. "How long do you think you
can keep this sort of thing up?" he asked. "This
will mean a great loss to the *News*."

Ed leaned back in his chair and looked into
Clark's eyes. "Clark, do you think if Jesus were
the editor of a paper he would print whiskey and
tobacco advertisements?"

"Well, no, I don't suppose he would," said
Clark. "But what has that got to do with us? We
can't do just as he would. Newspapers can't be
run like that. We'll lose more money than we
make!"

"Do you think so?" asked Ed, as if asking
himself. "I believe it's what Christ would do,
and as I told you, Clark, that's what I've promised to do for a year, no matter what happens to
me. I don't think we could ever say that Jesus
would print whiskey or tobacco ads in his newspaper. And there are other ads I'll have to look

I believe it's what Christ would do.

at and think about. Meanwhile, I must do what I feel I must.''

Clark went slowly back to his desk without speaking. Had his chief lost his mind? These new ideas would ruin the paper, he thought. It was just foolishness. Was Ed insane? Was he trying to destroy the whole business? Clark had always had great respect for his chief. But now . . . He shook his head and went down the stairs to tell Marks, the advertising agent, this new order.

On Friday of that week Ed faced his worst problem. On his desk were the pages for that week's Sunday paper. The *News* was one of the few evening papers in the city that had a Sunday edition, and it had been very successful. There was one page of literary and religious news to every thirty or forty pages of sports, theater, gossip, fashion, society, and politics. It made a very popular magazine.

Had his chief lost his mind?

But now Ed asked himself if Jesus would edit a Sunday paper. Would he put this reading material in thousands of homes every Sunday, a day that ought to be spent in something better and holier? True, it brought in a lot of money for the paper. Losing it would mean the loss of many thousands of dollars. And what about the customers who pay for a seven-day paper? He had no right to cheat them of reading material that they paid for.

But were any of these the real question? Wasn't the real question whether Jesus would edit or print a Sunday paper? As Ed sat there, struggling with these questions, he almost decided not to be guided by his new decision. So many things were involved, so many things could go wrong if he stopped the Sunday paper.

But then he decided. He went out of his office into the busy pressroom and called everyone to a

Ed asked himself if Jesus would edit a Sunday paper.

meeting. When everyone had gathered, Ed announced his decision not to run any more Sunday editions. The *News* would print a double edition on Saturday, he said, to make up the reading material to customers. No one at the paper would be hurt by the change, he promised. He would let all of the loss fall on himself. When he finished, everyone in the room was staring at him open-mouthed.

Clark followed him back into his office. Ed could tell by the look on Clark's face that he was upset — maybe to the point of quitting his job.

"You will ruin this paper in thirty days!" said Clark. "We might as well face that fact."

"I don't think we will," Ed said very calmly, but almost painfully. "But . . . will you stay until we do, Clark?"

Clark thought the smile on Ed's face seemed too peaceful, too confident, with everything that

*Everyone in the room was
staring at him.*

was happening. Was his chief really losing his mind? "Mr. Norman," he said, "I don't understand you. You're not the same man I've always known."

"I don't know myself either, Clark. Something remarkable has come over me, and it is carrying me on. But I have never been more convinced of final success and power for this paper. But you haven't answered my question. Will you stay with me?"

Clark stared at his chief, his friend, for a long time without speaking. Then, quietly and calmly, he said, "Yes."

Will you stay with me?

He stared at it in horror, unable to take his eyes from it.

4
Rachel Winslow

Alexander Powers, superintendent of the railroad shops, dropped the letter on his desk as if it were poison. He stared at it in horror, unable to take his eyes from it.

Just a few minutes ago he had sat down at his desk swelling with peace and contentment. Today was Monday of the second week since he had promised to follow in Christ's steps. All last week he had struggled with the question of what Jesus would do in his place. And he had come up with a plan to help the men who worked for him. He had set up a large, empty room near his office so the men could have a clean, quiet place to eat their lunch. He planned to put in reading tables and a coffeepot later. At his invitation, the

Reverend Henry Maxwell had come by today, to look over Alexander's plan and talk a little with the men during lunch. Henry had spoken very plainly and humbly, and those tough working men had taken to him almost as one of their own. Many had gone up to shake his hand before going back to work.

It was almost four o'clock when Henry finally left and Alexander sat down at his desk with a warm feeling in his heart. Somehow it seemed that his plan was, in some small way, something that Jesus might do.

But then he opened the letter. And he gasped. It was addressed to him, but the sender had clearly made a mistake. Alexander knew it was really meant for the superintendent of the freight department. Here before him was proof that the railroad company was cheating on freight and rebates. Alexander knew that the things detailed

Talk a little with the men during lunch.

in this letter were against the laws of the state and of the U.S. Interstate Commerce Laws. He dropped the letter on his desk and stared at it.

He had suspected for years that his company was breaking the laws like this. But nobody ever talked about it, and Alexander had always told himself it wasn't his business. Until now. Here was proof. This letter would convict the company of cheating on thousands of dollars. As soon as he had looked at the letter and realized what it meant, a question flashed through his mind: *What would Jesus do?* Would he ignore this, pretending it was none of his business? Or would he, as a member of a company that was breaking the law, turn them in?

Alexander knew what it might cost him to turn his company in. It could mean the loss of his comfortable job, the loss of all the luxuries he and his wife and daughter enjoyed, the loss of his

It could mean the loss of his comfortable job.

place in fashionable society. It might mean poverty, a whole new beginning. How could he possibly make his family suffer like that? Couldn't he just reseal the envelope and pretend he'd never seen it? Who would even know? After all, what business was it really of his, anyway? But what would Jesus do?

The clock on the wall ticked away the minutes, and the minutes became hours. Six o'clock quitting time came and went. The men in the shop had all gone home. Seven o'clock came, and the few remaining office managers had all gone. One office remained lighted. Kneeling by his desk, Alexander Powers was praying.

* * *

Earlier that day, Rachel Winslow had met her

One office remained lighted.

friend Virginia Page for lunch at the Page mansion. The two, both in their early twenties, had been good friends since they were children. Before lunch was served, they sat in Virginia's bedroom and talked of their choice to follow in Jesus' steps.

"I have decided to refuse this offer," Rachel said, holding a letter. It was from the manager of a comic opera, offering her a singing job with a large traveling musical company. The manager had been at the First Church two Sundays ago, where he heard Rachel sing. He had written her right away, offering her a very high salary.

"I'm convinced," continued Rachel, "that the Lord would never use a talent just to make money. But I have received another offer I'm not so sure about. It's with a very respected concert company, not at all like the comic opera. But, still, I'm not sure it's what Jesus would do. What

"I have decided to refuse this offer."

do you think?"

Virginia sighed and went over to the window overlooking the street below. "You mustn't ask me to decide for you," she said. "I'm having an even harder time than you in knowing what to do."

Rachel went to the window, and the two stood looking out at the busy street.

"I stand here and look out at all the poor humanity below, and I feel horror toward myself," said Virginia. "It maddens me to think that the society you and I have been brought up in is satisfied to go living and eating and dressing luxuriously, entertaining and being entertained. I can do anything I please, travel anywhere I want. I suppose many would envy me. But I feel as if I am one of the most wicked, selfish, useless creatures in all the world." Virginia turned from the window and began pacing the bedroom floor.

"I stand here and look out at all the poor humanity below.

The two were silent, each lost in her own thoughts, until lunch was announced.

It was during lunch that Rachel decided. She and Virginia were joined by Virginia's brother, Rollin, and her grandmother, Madam Page, an attractive and stately woman of sixty-five. Virginia's mother had died ten years ago, her father just last year. Madam Page, a shrewd businesswoman, now stayed with Rollin and Virginia.

Over lunch, Rollin and his grandmother pestered Rachel to tell of her plans. Would she accept either offer of a singing career? They continued to point out what a waste it would be if she didn't make a lot of money with her voice.

As they talked, Rachel grew certain of her choice. Finally she said, "I have decided not to accept either offer."

Madam Page looked stunned. "Would you

Would she accept either offer of a singing career?

mind telling us your reasons?'' she asked in her most important-sounding voice.

Her cheeks flushing, Rachel said, "Because I really believe Jesus Christ would do the same thing.''

Now Madam Page reddened, and Rollin just stared.

"Grandmother, you know how we promised not to do anything for one year without asking ourselves what Jesus would do?'' said Virginia.

"Of course!'' said Madam Page. "I understood Mr. Maxwell's proposition. And it is absurd!'' Now she looked very sharply at Virginia. "I have nothing to say of Miss Winslow's affairs, but I do hope you have no foolish notions in this matter, Virginia.''

"Excuse me, ladies,'' said Rollin. He looked embarrassed. "This conversation is getting beyond my depth.'' He left the room.

"Because I really believe Jesus Christ would do the same thing."

Now Madam Page looked keenly at both girls. "I am older by several years than you young ladies. I am telling you that what you have promised to do is utter foolishness. It is impossible. You will both see it in a different light after wiser thought." She rose to leave. "My dear Rachel, you will live to regret it if you do not accept the concert company's offer, or something like it." And after one last firm glance at the girls, she swished out of the room.

Rachel was glad when her visit was over and she was alone on the sidewalk. The walk home would give her time to gather her courage before facing her mother, who would be even worse than Madam Page.

But before she had gone two blocks, Rachel was startled to see Rollin at her side.

"Sorry to disturb your thoughts, Miss Winslow," he said, "but I happened to be going your

"My dear Rachel, you will live
to regret it.

way and thought you wouldn't object to my company." He smiled his rich-man smile and carelessly tossed his cigar into the street.

Rachel very much wanted to be alone, and she didn't like Rollin's manner. He was just a little older than Virginia, and Rachel had known him since they were children. But he had become snobbish and lazy, she thought, spending all his time at the rich gentlemen's clubs. Lately he had seemed to show a lot of interest in Rachel. Too much interest.

"Do you ever think of me?" he asked.

"Yes, I do," she said, a little impatiently.

"Are you thinking of me now?"

"Yes."

"What are you thinking?"

She hesitated. "Do you want the truth?"

"Of course."

He smiled his rich-man smile and carelessly tossed his cigar into the street.

"Then I was thinking that I wished you were not here."

Rollin bit his lip. "Now, look here! Oh, you know how I feel toward you. I've loved you for many years. I want you to be my wife. Is there any hope you might agree?"

"No," she said. She was annoyed now — annoyed to be proposed to on a busy, noisy street. She just wanted to be alone!

"Will you tell me why?" he asked, a little angrily.

"I don't love you. You have no purpose in life." She felt ready to burst into tears, and she couldn't stop herself from saying too much now. "What do you do to make the world better? You spend your life in luxury. What is there in a life like that to attract a woman?"

Rollin was looking down at the sidewalk now. "Not much, I guess," he said with a bitter laugh.

*What is there in a life like that
to attract a woman?*

"Still, I don't know that I'm any worse than the rest of the men around me. But I'm glad to know your reasons." He took off his hat, bowed gravely, and turned back.

Rachel hurried home. But now she was troubled. Was her judgment of Rollin fair? Was she any better? Up to that Sunday two weeks ago, she had thought of nothing but her singing career. Did she have any more purpose in life than Rollin?

She ran straight up to her room and lay on her bed. She did some very hard thinking, and some of her thoughts were painful. Finally she came to a decision.

"Mother, I have decided not to go out with the company," she said when she went downstairs. "I have a very good reason for it."

Her mother just stared at her as Rachel reminded her of her promise to follow Christ in

Finally she came to a decision.

everything.

"But what's that got to do with your decision?" her mother asked. "Do you mean to say that anyone with a singing career is wrong? Do you think you can judge others that way?"

This was even harder than Rachel had thought. Her mother had been hoping and planning for Rachel's singing career since Rachel was a little girl. She was very strong and determined. Rachel had never been able to stand up to her. "Please understand me," Rachel said. "I can't judge anyone else. I only know that I believe Jesus would have me do something else."

"What else?" asked her mother.

"Something that will serve mankind. Somewhere that the service of music is most needed. I have to feel satisfied that I am doing what I think Jesus would do in my place. I don't feel that way when I think of myself in a concert company

Do you think you can judge others that way?

career."

Her mother's eyes flashed. Her voice was icy. "Rachel, you are a fanatic! This is absurd! What can you do?"

"Mother, not everyone with a natural talent seeks money or fame. Some choose to serve with it instead. I have decided to continue to sing at the church on Sundays. During the week I will sing at the White Cross meetings, down in the Rectangle, as they have asked me to."

Her mother's face suddenly turned pale. "What?" she cried. "Rachel Winslow! Do you know what you are saying? Do you know what sort of people are down there?"

Inside, Rachel was trembling. But she faced her mother with as brave a look as she could manage. "I know very well what sort of people are down there," she said. "That is the reason I am going. In fact, I am going tonight."

Do you know what sort of people are down there?

RACHEL WINSLOW

Back upstairs, her heart pounding, Rachel knelt by her bed and prayed. A long time later, when she arose, her face was wet with tears.

* * *

The big white tent stood in the middle of the barren field, amid straggling weeds and broken whiskey bottles and faded circus posters trampled into the hard-packed dirt by the passing of thousands of unfeeling feet. On either side of the field, stretching endlessly into the darkness, were rows of noisy, stinking saloons, gambling houses, pool halls, and cheap, dirty boarding houses. Beyond these, the giant smokestacks of the great railroad shops rose up into the sooty night sky.

This was the Rectangle, an abandoned field

The big white tent stood in the middle of the barren field.

used sometimes in summer by traveling circuses and wandering showmen. Just a couple of weeks ago a traveling evangelist named John Gray and his wife had set up their tent and begun holding meetings every night.

Tonight a new sound came from the tent. Here and there a dark window in a dark house opened and a face peered out. A man reeling down the sidewalk with a bottle in his hand stopped and turned in the direction of the tent. Two men cursing and shoving each other in a doorway stopped suddenly and listened.

Someone was singing. Her soft voice drifted out of the tent, across the Rectangle, into the streets. It was like an angel's voice.

Alexander Powers heard the voice, too. He was coming home this way tonight, having stayed late in his office, praying, struggling to decide what to do about the letter. Now he

It was like an Angel's voice.

recognized Rachel's voice. "Where he leads me I will follow. I'll go with him all the way." He stopped at a street corner, listening.

As he stood there, a tear rolled down his cheek. Before he turned to go on his way again, both cheeks were wet. He had his answer. He knew what he must do.

As he stood there, a tear rolled down his cheek.

He felt so different from these people.

5
"I Come"

Wednesday night at the Rectangle, the tent was crowded. The night was mild, the tent sides drawn up, and faces stared in from outside, all around the tent.

Henry Maxwell was here tonight. John Gray asked him to speak tonight, because John had a cold. Henry had said yes humbly, and the two of them had kneeled in Henry's study to pray.

Henry was almost terrified to be speaking here tonight. He felt so different from these people — these crude, drunken Rectangle people. But he knew in his heart that his Lord was calling him to reach out in love to these people.

Just tonight he had sat in his study and written a list of what he thought Jesus would want him to do in his life as a minister. He realized that his list went completely against his habits in the First Church. He knew he must live simply, with no needless luxuries. He must preach against the saloons in Raymond, preach fearlessly to hypocrites in his church, no matter how important they were in the community. And he must become a friend to the lost, dying people everywhere — in his church and in the Rectangle.

So here he was. When he was introduced he stood up trembling. He said a few words and someone in the back laughed loudly. Then others started talking, some shouting. Many seemed drunk. Some began shouting, "Song! Song! Give us a song!" Henry turned to Rachel Winslow, who was sitting behind him. "Sing something, please," he said. "They will listen to you." He sat down and covered his face with his hands.

Sing something, please.

"I COME"

Virginia Page began playing the organ, and Rachel sang. "Savior, I follow on, guided by thee, seeing not yet the hand that leadeth me."

Everyone was suddenly quiet. This was what they wanted. Hard, twisted faces softened. Eyes grew glazed, staring into memories. Here and there a tear rolled down a beard-stubbled cheek. When Rachel finished, peace had settled on the tent.

Now Henry spoke. As he spoke, love grew in his heart for these people, a love deeper and more pure than any he had ever known. These were the people Jesus died for. He spoke clearly and plainly of Christ's dying to save us from sin.

When the meeting was over, everyone drifted out of the tent, across the bristly field, and back into the rows. Life at the Rectangle — the drinking, the gambling, the sin — would go on as always, on into the night.

"Love grew in his heart for these people."

"I COME"

Henry walked home with Rachel, Virginia, and Jasper Chase, past the saloons and dark doors to the corner where carriages passed by. "This is a terrible spot," said Henry. "I never realized that Raymond had such a festering sore. It doesn't seem possible that this is a city full of Christian disciples." He was staring back at the tent. It looked very white, very clean in the darkness of the Rectangle.

The next night, Henry was in his study, reading that night's *Daily News*. He was pleased with what he read. Ed Norman was clearly keeping his promise to follow Jesus. Over the past two weeks, the paper had taken on a whole new look. There were no more detailed reports of crimes, no more scandal or gossip, no more liquor or tobacco advertisements. There was just good, solid news, and the writing even seemed better.

Suddenly Henry stood up. "Listen to this,

He was pleased with what he read.

Mary!" he said to his wife. His hand shook a bit as he read her an account of Alexander Powers, who had turned in the railroad company for violation of state and federal laws. Powers had lost his job because of his action, the report said.

Henry dropped the paper. "I must go see Powers," he said. As he was going out the door, Mary said, "Henry, do you think Jesus would have done that?"

Henry paused with his hand on the door. "Yes, I think he would," he said slowly.

"How about his family? How will Mrs. Powers and Celia take it?"

"Very hard, no doubt. That will be his cross to carry in this. They won't understand him at all."

Alexander lived only a block from Henry. They shook hands at the door and went in. After they had talked a while, Alexander said, "There is one thing I would like you to do. As far as I

"*Henry, do you think Jesus would have done that?*"

know, the company won't object to the thing I started with the lunchroom and all. Would you see to it that that work goes on? Maybe you could go down there sometimes and talk to the men."

Henry promised he would. Then the two men prayed together. When they parted, Henry's firm handshake and warm smile told Alexander that his pastor was proud of him.

As he walked home, Henry thought of all the things that had happened in the short two weeks since he had asked for volunteers to follow in Jesus' steps. He was just beginning to see something of what it costs to be a true disciple of Jesus Christ. But he could not see the hundreds and thousands of lives that would be changed — not just in Raymond, but in the whole country.

*　　*　　*

"His pastor was proud of him."

"I COME"

There was something different about this Saturday night at the Rectangle. The tent was full as usual, and even more people stood outside. But tonight, for the first time, the people had all come in quietly and waited to hear the message. All these weeks of nightly meetings, all the nights that Mr. Gray and his wife and the few volunteers from the First Church had come here, had finally shown these Rectangle people that here, at last, was love. Here was real love that did not quit, did not go away. Here was God. Tonight the people listened, expecting, hoping. And as Rachel sang, Mr. Gray made a small gesture. *Come.* Come and meet the Lord Jesus Christ. Come and be made clean, be made new.

And they came. The whole mass of people, it seemed, moved toward the front. "Just as I am, without one plea, but that thy blood was shed for me. And that thou bidst me come to thee, O

Come and be made clean, be made new.

"I COME"

Lamb of God, I come, I come." Rachel's sweet voice hovered in the air, melting hearts, bending knees to the ground.

Virginia, playing the organ, couldn't take her eyes off one woman standing nearby. On the woman's face was such sadness, such desperate sadness, that Virginia's heart ached. She got up from the organ and went to the woman, taking her face in her hands. Weeping, the woman sank to her knees, bowing her head onto a wooden bench. And Virginia, with her face next to the woman's, prayed and wept with her.

"I come. I come."

Rachel, noticing someone dressed in fine, expensive clothing kneeling near her, looked down. Her voice faltered for an instant. There, kneeling and weeping shoulder to shoulder with a man wearing a torn, stained coat and smelling of stale whiskey, was Rollin Page! "I come. I come."

And Virginia, with her face
next to the woman's prayed and
wept with her.

He preached against sin.

6
The Battle Begins

The next morning held the strangest Sunday service the people of First Church could remember. Gone was Henry's smooth, eloquent style of speaking. Gone were his soothing words of encouragement and comfort. Gone even were the notes he had always read from. Today he spoke humbly and plainly. He preached against sin, against hypocrisy, against rich, comfortable Christians ignoring the poor, starving people of Raymond. And he preached against the saloons in Raymond. He reminded his listeners that the city elections were coming up soon. The Christian thing to do, he said, would be to gather together to fight the laws that permitted the saloon business and to elect good, responsible

119

men to fight this evil.

Henry didn't know what effect his preaching had. He was simply doing what he believed his Lord had told him to do. But after the service he was startled to find over a hundred people gathered in the lecture room — people who had decided to follow in Jesus' steps.

There was a lot of excitement in the lecture room today. The talk was of the amazing changes in the *Daily News,* of Alexander Powers's turning in the railroad company for fraud and losing his job, of Milton Wright, owner of several large stores citywide, and the wonderful changes everyone noticed in his stores — changes made because of Milton's decision to run his businesses the way he thought Jesus would.

After the meeting, Donald Marsh, president of Lincoln College, walked home with Henry.

There was a lot of excitement in the lecture room today.

Donald appeared lost in thought. Finally he said, "Your sermon today has made clear to me how I am to follow Jesus. I have known for a long time what I must do, but I have so dreaded the thought that I have tried hard to ignore it. But I can't any longer. It will be the cross that I have to bear. You may be able to guess what it is."

"Yes, I think I know," said Henry. "It is my cross, too. I would rather do anything besides this."

Donald smiled. Then he said, sadly, "Henry, you and I belong to a class of professional men who have always avoided public life. We have lived in a world of books and seclusion, doing work we enjoy and ignoring our duties as citizens. I confess with shame that I have avoided the responsibility that I owe this city. I know that our city officials are corrupt and selfish, controlled by the big money of the liquor business in this

I owe this city.

city. Yet all these years I have let these men run this city, running it into ruin, and I have done nothing. My plain duty is to take part in this coming election, to do whatever is in my power to elect good men who will stand up to the evil corruption in this city. And I tell you, I would rather walk up to the mouth of a cannon than do this. I dread the touch of it. I hate everything to do with politics. But I am convinced that this is what Jesus would have me do. It will cost me, I know. But it is clear to me that I must suffer this, or else deny my Lord."

They walked on in silence for a while. Then Henry said, "You have spoken for me also. As a minister I have sheltered myself from my duties as a citizen. Donald, men like you and me — ministers, professors, artists, writers, scholars — have almost always been political cowards. We love our world of thought and study and are too

You have spoken for me also.

comfortable there to come out into public life, into a society that is evil, that stinks, that is rotting in its selfishness and sin. But I, like you, know that if my Lord calls me I must follow him.''

Donald stopped suddenly and laid a hand on Henry's shoulder. There was a new light in his eyes. "We need not act alone!" he said. "With all the people in our church who have made this promise, we can organize the Christian forces in Raymond against liquor and political corruption. Let's organize a campaign that will really mean something! If we must bear this cross, let's at least do so bravely, like men.''

They walked on, making plans and growing more and more excited.

* * *

They walked on, making plans and growing more and more excited.

THE BATTLE BEGINS

That Friday night the city primaries were held at the courthouse. At this public meeting, the people were nominated, by vote, to run for office. The offices up for election were mayor, city council, chief of police, city clerk, and city treasurer. But this meeting was not like any the city had ever known.

Saturday's *Daily News* carried the story in Ed Norman's editorial. "Never before in the history of Raymond was there a primary like last night's," the story read. "It came as a complete surprise to the city politicians who have been in the habit of running this city as if they owned it. But they were overwhelmingly surprised last night as a large number of citizens entered the primary and controlled it, nominating some of the best men for all the offices in the coming election.

"It was a tremendous lesson in good citizenship," the story continued. "President Marsh of

*"It came as a complete surprise
to the city politicians."*

THE BATTLE BEGINS

Lincoln College, who was completely unknown to the city politicians, gave one of the best speeches ever heard in Raymond. The old-time ring of city rulers was clearly outnumbered. In disgust, they withdrew and nominated another ticket. This last ticket contains the names of whiskey men. The line in this election is clearly drawn between the saloon owners and corrupt city management, as we have known for years, and a clean, honest, and capable administration, such as every good citizen should want. This will be the most important question in this election. This city has reached its crisis. The question to us now is, shall we continue the rule of liquor and shameless corruption, or begin a new order of cleansing our city?

"The *News* is positively on the side of the new movement. We will do everything in our power to drive out the saloons and destroy their political

"One of the best speeches ever heard in Raymond."

strength. We call on all Christians to stand by
President Marsh and the rest of the citizens who
have begun this reform.''

*　　*　　*

A week later, Saturday afternoon, Virginia
stepped out of her house to go visit Rachel. As
she walked, she thought about Ed's editorial of
last week. She felt a joy that she had not felt for
these past few weeks. Virginia was quickly coming to a decision about what to do with a good
part of her money. It was clear that Ed Norman
had lost a lot of money because of his actions in
the newspaper. He had lost a lot of subscribers
and advertisers. This latest editorial would mean
even more loss, she knew. The *News* would be
the only paper in Raymond to stand against the

Virginia stepped out of her house to go visit Rachel.

whiskey people. This political battle could ruin the paper. Could it survive if enough good people in Raymond supported it? Could it prosper and grow if Ed Norman had the money he needed to start the new plans he had told the group in the lecture room about last Sunday? What if someone were to donate, say, half a million dollars? Virginia could hardly keep from laughing out loud as she thought about these things.

Just then a carriage pulled up. Three of her friends were out for an afternoon drive, dressed in their finest. "Where have you been all this time, Virginia?" asked one of the girls, tapping her playfully on the shoulder with a red silk parasol. "We heard you've gone into show business." The three laughed. "Tell us all about it."

Virginia's face flushed. But she told the girls

Just then a carriage pulled up.

briefly of her experiences at the Rectangle.

"Girls!" one of the three said. "Let's go slumming with Virginia this afternoon, instead of to the band concert. I've never seen the Rectangle. I hear it's an awful place, with lots to see." She was smiling with delight.

"Oh, yes, let's!" the other two said.

Virginia was angry. These girls didn't know what they were saying. They had never seen that side of Raymond, never seen the human sin and suffering of the Rectangle. *But let them see it,* she thought. "All right, I'll take you," she said, and climbed into the carriage.

"Shouldn't we take a policeman?" asked one of the girls with a nervous laugh. "It really isn't safe down there, you know."

"There's no danger," said Virginia.

"Is it true that your brother Rollin has been converted?" asked another one.

"*Girls ... Let's go slumming with Virginia this afternoon.*"

"Yes, he certainly has."

"I hear he's going to the clubs trying to preach to his old friends. Isn't that funny?" said the one with the red parasol. The others laughed with her.

But then the carriage turned a corner and started down the street into the Rectangle district. None of the girls laughed now. As the sights and sounds and smells of the Rectangle struck them, the girls began to look pale. Everyone in the street, in the saloon doorways, hanging out of windows, stared at the fine carriage with the fashionable young society girls from uptown.

"Let's go back!" said one of the girls. "I've seen enough."

Suddenly a young woman stumbled out of the doorway of a large gambling house. She reeled into the street, singing at the top of her voice,

None of the girls laughed now.

THE BATTLE BEGINS

"Just as I am, without one plea . . ."

"Stop!" cried Virginia. It was the woman from the tent meeting last week, the one Virginia had prayed with. The woman had confessed her sins and had come to believe in the Lord. Now here she was again, sloppy drunk.

Virginia jumped down from the carriage and ran to the woman. "Loreen!" she cried.

Virginia's friends in the carriage looked on in horror. Their good friend Virginia was standing there amid the gathering onlookers with her arm around the drunken woman's shoulders! What had come over Virginia?

"Drive on," Virginia said. "I'm going to see my friend home."

The girl with the red parasol gasped. Her *friend!* "Can't we — that is — do you want our help?"

"No!" said Virginia. "You cannot be of any help to me."

"I'm going to see my friend home."

THE BATTLE BEGINS

The carriage pulled away. Virginia looked around her. Not all the faces were hard and cruel. Some looked on with sympathy, even with sadness. *The Lord has truly been doing a work here,* Virginia thought.

Suddenly the woman wrenched herself free from Virginia. "Don't touch me!" she screamed. "Leave me alone! Let me go to hell, where I belong. The devil is waiting for me. See him? She pointed a wavering finger at the fat, unshaven saloonkeeper standing in his doorway, a sneer on his face. The crowd laughed. But not all of the crowd. A few turned and walked away with their heads down.

"Loreen!" said Virginia, taking the woman by the shoulders. "You do not belong in hell! You belong to Jesus, and he will save you. Come, Loreen. I want to take you to Mr. Gray's."

But the Grays were not home. Loreen sank to

The devil is waiting for me.
See him?

the sidewalk in front of the Grays' doorstep, sobbing. What could Virginia do? Suddenly the thought struck her. Why not take Loreen home? Surely that's what Jesus would do.

And that's what Virginia did.

Madam Page glared at Virginia and clenched her hands as the two young ladies stood in the hallway of the Page mansion. Loreen was almost passed out now, leaning heavily on Virginia.

"Virginia!" her grandmother hissed. "Do you know what that girl is?"

"I know very well," said Virginia. "She is an outcast. But she is also a child of God. I have seen her on her knees, repentant. By the grace of Christ, the least I can do is rescue her from slipping back into peril. I must keep her here tonight, and longer if necessary."

"Then you can answer for the consequences! I will not stay in the same house with this — this

"Do you know what that girl is?"

miserable —'' Madam Page was too furious to speak.

"Grandmother, this house is mine. It is yours, too, as long as you choose to stay. But I must act as I fully believe Jesus would in my place. And I am willing to answer for the consequences, no matter what society may say or do. Society is not my God. Compared to this poor soul, the judgment of society is worthless.''

"I shall not stay here, then!'' said Madam Page. "And you can always remember that you have driven your grandmother out of your home in favor of a drunken woman!'' She was so angry that the color had left her face. She threw up her chin and turned toward the door.

Virginia couldn't pay any more attention to her grandmother. Loreen was collapsing. Virginia cried out for a servant. A housemaid came running down the hall, wiping her hands on

Virginia cried out for a servant.

a dish towel. Together they got Loreen to Virginia's room and onto the bed.

Dr. West came that night to examine Loreen. She would sleep it off, he said, and would be all right. So Loreen lay there that night in Virginia's beautiful bed while Virginia sat by the bed, rocking and watching her. Virginia was hurt by the scene that afternoon with her grandmother, but she had no doubt that this is what Jesus would do. Rocking and praying and watching, she fell asleep.

Rocking and praying and watching, she fell asleep.

Today the drinking was heavier than usual.

7
Murder At the Rectangle

It was the next Saturday, election day. All that week, Donald Marsh, Henry Maxwell, and others had been very busy going about the city, speaking against the saloons and urging people to vote the whiskey men out of office. It was the hardest week that either Donald or Henry had ever lived. Every night they would go home exhausted. And they spent a lot of time in prayer, asking God for strength.

Now the week was over. Tonight would decide whether they had won or not. If they did win, all the saloons in the Rectangle would soon be closed.

Today the drinking was heavier than usual. All the worst of Raymond, it seemed, gathered in the saloons and gambling houses and pool halls of the

Rectangle. They drank and drank and cursed the Christians who had dared to speak against the saloons of Raymond.

The election polls closed at six o'clock. Now the votes would be counted. Tonight would tell.

John Gray had almost decided to cancel the tent meeting that night. But then he felt the Lord's gentle prompting and went ahead as usual. President Marsh had come with Henry Maxwell. Dr. West and Rollin Page had also come with Virginia and Rachel. And Loreen, who had stayed with Virginia that week, sat next to Virginia at the organ, like a child afraid to leave her mother's side.

The tent was full, as usual. Rachel's singing was as beautiful as ever.

But tonight was different. A new energy was in the air. It came creeping across the bare field from the streets, the saloons, the smoke-filled

A new energy was in the air.

gambling houses, from the gaping, rotting boarding houses. The Rectangle people had come swarming out into the streets, like rats from their dark, dank hiding places. And they were full of drunken hatred tonight.

Mr. Gray closed the service early, and the people slowly emptied out of the tent. Rachel, Virginia, Loreen, Rollin, Dr. West, Donald, and Henry left together as soon as they could get away. They had to go down the street through the worst of the Rectangle. The crowd seemed on the verge of a riot. As the group of friends pushed their way through the crowds, a rough voice shouted, "There he is! The bloke in the tall hat! He's the leader."

"Marsh, we're in trouble here!" said Henry sharply. "We must get the ladies to a safe place."

Donald nodded grimly. Now they were hemmed

"There he is! The bloke
in the tall hat! He's
the leader."

in by the crowd. The narrow street and sidewalk in front of them were completely choked with reeling, cursing, angry people.

Suddenly from behind came a shower of stones and mud and empty whiskey bottles. "Down with the aristocrats!" came a shrill voice. Quickly the men in the little group surrounded the three women as more stones and mud came flying. Rollin jumped in front of Rachel just as a heavy chunk of brick came out of the mob, straight toward her. It thudded off his chest, staggering him. He stood his ground, shielding her with his arms out. Another stone hit him in the face, and another.

"Virginia!" Loreen screamed. "Look out!" She leaped toward Virginia and shoved her, just as a heavy bottle dropped from a second-story window. It smashed on Loreen's head, knocking her facedown onto the sidewalk.

A heavy bottle dropped from a second-story window.

Just then a policeman's whistle shrieked over the clamor. Half a dozen policemen surged through the mob toward the little group, swinging nightsticks as they came.

Donald Marsh raised his hand and shouted, "Stop! You have killed a woman!"

A hush fell over the mob. Suddenly everyone was scurrying off the street, darting into dark corners and doorways. Soon the street was deserted except for the little group and the policemen, all standing in a silent circle around Loreen.

Virginia was kneeling over Loreen, holding her head in her lap and weeping. Dr. West was on the other side of her, gently feeling the wound on her head. He looked up helplessly. "She's dying," he said very quietly.

Loreen opened her eyes and looked up, smiling, into Virginia's face. Virginia gently wiped blood

*All standing in a silent circle
around Loreen.*

off Loreen's face with her silk handkerchief, bent over slowly, and kissed her on the forehead. And Loreen, smiling up at her friend Virginia, the only friend she had ever known, slowly closed her eyes. She had at last found peace, joy, and freedom.

*   *   *

On Sunday morning Henry Maxwell stood before his people of the First Church. There was no smile on his face today, only bandages from his adventure at the Rectangle the night before.

The news had spread quickly over the city this morning: The people of Raymond had voted for whiskey.

Henry stepped away from the pulpit and walked down in front of the aisles. A look of

There was no smile on his face today.

something like sorrow was on his face.

"The Christians of Raymond stand condemned by this vote," he said. "Many professing Christians did not vote yesterday, and many more voted for the whiskey men. If all the church members in Raymond had voted against the saloons, today they would be outlawed, instead of crowned king of this city.

"And this woman who was brutally struck down by the very hand that worked her earthly ruin — what of her? For another year, at least, this very saloon that received her so often, from whose very spot the weapon was hurled that struck her dead, will open its door daily to a hundred more like her."

He was not ashamed to weep as he spoke. His voice rang out and trembled and broke in sobs.

The faces in the congregation today were grim. One by one, the people began weeping. President

He was not ashamed to weep as he spoke.

Marsh sat with his head bowed, tears rolling down his cheeks. Ed Norman sat staring at the ceiling, his lips trembling, his hand clutching the end of his pew. Up in the choir loft, Rachel Winslow had bowed her head on the railing as sobs gently shook her body. Today would be the first Sunday that she would not be able to sing her solo.

And in the great hallway of the Page mansion, in a casket covered with a rich cloth, lay the body of Loreen, awaiting her funeral.

But where she was now, she was not weeping. She would never have to weep again.

Ed Norman sat staring at the ceiling

"I am going to do something with my money."

8
Rachel and Rollin

It was the day after Loreen's funeral. Virginia and Rachel sat in the hallway of the Page mansion.

"I don't know if anyone in Raymond has felt Loreen's death more keenly than I have, Rachel," said Virginia, looking into her friend's eyes. "That short week that she stayed with me opened my heart to a whole new life." Her eyes were moist. Her hands, folded on her lap, trembled slightly. She took a deep breath.

"I am going to do something with my money to help those Rectangle women to a better life," she said. She looked toward the end of the hall, where Loreen's body had lain. "I have talked about it with Rollin. He will devote a large part of his money to the same plan.''

"What about your plan to give money to Ed Norman's newspaper?'' asked Rachel.

"I have already arranged everything with Mr. Norman,'' said Virginia. "His plan is wonderful. Raymond desperately needs a Christian daily paper like the one he plans to develop. I have perfect confidence in his ability to make it work.

"But I still have over half a million dollars. And I know now how to use it." She suddenly took Rachel's hands. The look on her face was now one of eagerness and excitement. "Rachel, I want you to work with me. Rollin and I are going to buy a large part of the property in the Rectangle. I have been studying various forms of college settlements and Christian residence centers in city slums. I don't know how to do all of this, of course, but I want to build good, wholesome lodging houses for poor, lost girls like Loreen.

"*Rachel, I want you to work with me.*"

"And now for your part," she continued, her face beaming. "Your voice is a power for God, Rachel. I've had many ideas lately. One of them is that you could organize a musical institute for girls. You will have the best organs and orchestras that money can buy. Oh, Rachel, think of what music can do there to win souls to higher, purer, better living!"

Rachel was in a trance. Her face shined as this new vision of her life's work dawned on her. She rose, Virginia with her, and they embraced. "Yes," Rachel said. "Yes, I will gladly put my life into that kind of service. I do believe that Jesus would have me use my life this way. Virginia, think what miracles can be performed with your money, and, and —"

"And your enthusiasm," Virginia said with a laugh. "And, of course, your voice."

Just then Rollin came into the hall, and Virginia

Your voice is a power for God.

called him. The three talked for a little while over their plan. When Rollin had gone out again, Virginia turned to Rachel.

"By the way, what has become of Jasper Chase? I suppose he is writing another novel. You know, I could tell that he made the heroine in his first book just like you. He made his feelings for you pretty clear, I think."

A cloud came over Rachel's face. "Virginia, Jasper told me the other night, walking home from the Rectangle meeting, that he — in fact, he proposed to me — or he would have, if —" Her eyes suddenly filled with tears.

"Virginia, a little while ago, I thought I loved him. But that was before my experiences at the Rectangle, before I made such a deep commitment to follow Jesus. And that first night at the tent meeting, when all those people gave their hearts to the Lord . . . It seemed to mean nothing

Her eyes suddenly filled with tears.

to Jasper. He said he cared only for me. I have been so caught up with the Lord, with my new feelings as his disciple, that when Jasper spoke to me, I was suddenly repelled. I refused him. I'm sure I don't love him, and that I never really did. He touched my emotions with his novel, and I was very flattered. But I do not love him. Not enough to give him my life.''

Virginia just sat there quietly, listening, a tender smile slowly growing. ''Rachel, I'm glad for you,'' she said softly.

Rachel looked startled. ''You are? Why?''

''Because I have never really liked Jasper Chase. He seems so cold. Although I don't like to judge anyone, I always doubted his sincerity about taking the pledge at church with the rest of us. And have you noticed that he has stopped coming to our meetings after the service in the lecture room?''

"Rachel, I'm glad for you."

RACHEL AND ROLLIN

Rachel was looking down at the floor. When she looked up, there were tears in her friend's eyes. They embraced again, closer friends than they had ever been.

*   *   *

Two months passed. The heat of summer settled over the city. The Grays had packed up and moved on to find other places to save lost souls. From the outside, life at the Rectangle looked no different, though hundreds of lives had been changed by those tent meetings.

On a warm August afternoon, Rollin Page walked out of his house and down the sidewalk on his way to one of his clubs. He turned a corner and almost ran into Rachel. On seeing her, his heart beat faster. They greeted each other and

On seeing her, his heart beat faster.

walked on together.

They chatted about the new work going on at the Rectangle, the First Church, and other things. But Rachel was not comfortable. She wondered why Rollin had become so different with her since his conversion at the Rectangle. Lately he seemed to avoid her as much as possible, and when they did speak, he was very formal and polite, never saying anything about himself or asking her about herself.

She looked at him with a new curiosity. "What have you been doing all summer?" she asked. "I haven't seen much of you." Suddenly her cheeks flushed, and she quickly looked away.

"I have been busy," he said quickly.

"Tell me something about it," she said. "You say so little. Do I have a right to ask?" She realized her heart was beating faster. Was she saying too much? What were her feelings about this

*She realized her heart was
beating faster.*

man, anyway? He was so different from the Rollin she used to know. He seemed much nobler, more manly, much more gracious. There was none of his old look of smugness, none of his old proud, haughty look. This was truly a changed man.

"I'm not so certain I can tell you much," he said slowly. "I have been going to the clubs, as I used to. But I have been trying to lead the men into more useful lives. You see, I am not suited to work in the Rectangle. I just don't fit. I asked myself many times what Jesus would do. And it seems that my answer is to do as I am, that is, to try to reach the men I know. Actually, some of them have responded very well, giving up old habits. I'm still feeling my way, of course, and I'm not always sure of what I should do. I am merely experiencing all the newness of life as a brand-new Christian."

You see, I am not suited to work in the Rectangle.

As he talked, his tone became more excited. He was clearly a man with a mission in life, Rachel thought.

Now they passed the spot where Rollin had proposed to Rachel a few months ago. Both suddenly became shy. Rachel turned to Rollin and looked into his face. "Do you remember when I told you that you had no purpose in life?" she asked.

He looked down at the sidewalk.

"I want to say," Rachel continued, "that I . . . I need to say that I honor you now for your courage and your obedience to the promise you have made. The life you are living is a noble one."

Rollin looked up slowly. His eyes met hers. "Thank you," he said. "It's worth more to me than I can say to hear you say that."

As their eyes met briefly, Rachel could read love for her in his gaze.

Rachel could read love for her in his gaze.

RACHEL AND ROLLIN

Soon they reached Rachel's house and said good-bye.

Upstairs in her room, Rachel sat down at her dressing table and put her face in her hands. She hadn't realized that her hands were shaking. "I am beginning to know what it means to be loved by a noble man," she said out loud. "I will love Rollin Page after all."

She stood up quickly and began pacing the floor. She didn't understand this new feeling. But as she paced, she began to realize that this feeling didn't frighten her. It made her want to weep with gladness. It was too big for her heart to hold. Her heart felt ready to burst. With joy!

As Rollin went on his way down the sidewalk, a new hope sprang up in his heart, a hope that had died during his old life, a hope he had not dared to have in his new life. But here it was!

"I will love Rollin Page after all."

Dr. Calvin Bruce, pastor of the Nazareth Avenue Church

9
The Dawn

A year had passed. It was late Sunday night. A light was shining from a third-story window in the downtown hotel in Raymond. Dr. Calvin Bruce, pastor of the Nazareth Avenue Church in Chicago, was in his room writing a letter.

"My dear Craxton,

"It is late, but I am so intensely awake and so overflowing with what I have seen and heard this week that I feel I must write you.

"As I told you, I have been visiting some friends this week in Raymond, including Henry Maxwell, whom you will remember as one of our old classmates in seminary. As you probably remember, he was a very refined, scholarly fellow, who was a very good speaker, and who wrote beautiful, even elegant sermons. Do you remember when the First Church of Raymond chose him as their pastor? I said then that they had made a very good choice. The people there, mostly well-to-do folk from the best parts of town, would be very pleased with Henry, I said."

Dr. Bruce was writing very quickly, as if he couldn't write fast enough to keep up with his thoughts.

"But a year ago today," he continued, "as you've heard, Maxwell made the astonishing challenge to his members to volunteer for a year not to do anything without first asking the question, what would Jesus do? And some of the results of this I need not even tell you of, as the whole country has heard of them. You know about the *Daily News,* the Christian paper that editor Edward Norman has turned into a powerful force in this city, and that has already made

Dr. Bruce was writing very quickly.

such a sensation in the newspaper world. Milton Wright, owner of several stores here, who has become one of the most beloved men in this city in one short year because of changing his business policies to suit what he believes Jesus would do. Alexander Powers, whose action in the federal court against the L & T railroad company made national headlines last year. I have heard that as a result of this action, the president of L & T has resigned and is facing criminal charges. The company itself will soon be turned over to new management.

"You have heard too, I'm sure, of Rachel Winslow, whose singing has made her nationally known. She has dedicated her life to a great reform movement in the slum area called the Rectangle. This work is incredible, Craxton! Already there are several buildings constructed in an old abandoned field. The plan was created by one of

This work is incredible, Craxton!

the city's leading society heiresses, a Miss Virginia Page, said to be a good friend of Miss Winslow's. Miss Page has dedicated her whole fortune to the plan, which is for a center for young women.

"Other churches in this city have taken this pledge, too, and there are now literally hundreds of Christians actively living their lives as the members of the First Church have done this year.

"And Donald March, president of Lincoln College, is very active this year, as I'm told he was last year, in the coming city elections. The Christians in this city are fighting to get the whiskey men out of office, to close all the saloons in that area called the Rectangle. The whiskey men had a very tough time winning last year, I've heard, and this year their defeat looks certain.

"Oh, yes, I don't want to forget this part. Old as I am, I am not too old to be interested in the

"And Donald March, president of Lincoln College, is very active this year"

romantic side of life. I must tell you that it is well understood that Miss Winslow expects to be married this spring to a Mr. Rollin Page, brother of Miss Winslow's friend Virginia. They are a beautiful couple, Craxton. It would do your old heart good, as it has mine, to see two young people so in love and so dedicated to serving Christ with their lives.''

Dr. Bruce paused here to look out his window a bit, smiling, with a faraway look on his face. He took a deep breath and began writing again on a fresh sheet of paper.

"But the effect on Maxwell is the most remarkable of all," he wrote. "The last time I heard him preach, about four years ago, was typical of his sermons. What we used to call 'pleasing' in seminary, you remember? But this morning I visited the First Church and heard him again. And I tell you, Craxton, he is not the same

Miss Winslow expects to be married this spring to Mr. Rollin Page.

man! He gives me the impression of someone
who has gone through a crisis. He spoke of his
idea that Christians must make a clear commitment to follow Jesus, especially to suffer somehow as Christ did. He is convinced that what the
Christian church needs today is some sort of
joyful suffering for Christ. But as I said, his sermon today was so far different from the old
Maxwell. I was really touched, as I have never
been. I actually shed tears once, and I noticed
that many others did too. After the service he
asked me to join his group in the lecture room.
These are the people who have pledged to follow
Christ. They meet every Sunday like this.
Nothing in all my minister's life, Craxton,
moved me so much as that meeting. I have never
felt the Spirit so powerfully. I thought back to
what it must have been like in the earliest days of
Christianity. This meeting was what I imagine

I have never felt the Spirit so powerfully.

that to have been — so simple, so honest, so humble, so pure was everyone's expression of childlike faith in Christ. I never dreamed that such Christian fellowship could exist in this age.

"But now, dear friend, I come to the real purpose of this letter. At the meeting today, Maxwell and his people took steps to plan for a calling of all Christian churches in the nation to take an honest look at themselves and ask themselves if they are ready to follow in Christ's steps in this way. 'Suppose," he said, 'that church memberships throughout the country made this pledge and lived up to it! What a revelation it would cause for Christianity! But why not? Is it really any more than a disciple of Christ's should do? Unless a person is willing to do this, has he really followed Christ? Is the test of being a true disciple any less today than in Jesus' time?' Maxwell asked. The members of the First Church, I can

"*But now, dear friend, I come to the real purpose of this letter.*"

tell you, are convinced that the time has come to fellowship with other Christians in this way.

"This is a grand idea, Craxton, but right here is where I find myself hesitating. I don't deny that the Christian disciple ought to follow Christ's steps as closely as these here in Raymond have tried to do. But I can't avoid asking what the result would be if I asked my church in Chicago to do it. I am writing this after having felt the powerful touch of the Holy Spirit's presence, and I confess to you, old friend, that I cannot think of even a dozen people in my church who would make this pledge at the risk of everything they own and of their reputations. Can you do any better in your church? What would we say if we failed, Craxton? You know, the results of the pledge as obeyed here in Raymond are enough to make any pastor tremble, and at the same time to make him long with yearning that

What the result would be if I asked my church in Chicago to do it.

they might happen in his own church.

"My church is full of wealthy, satisfied people. They have no idea, I know, of what it means to suffer. I wonder, do they really have any idea, then, how much Jesus Christ suffered for us? And do I? Perhaps I haven't understood it myself, Craxton. Perhaps I haven't ever stirred these feelings in my people because I myself haven't been faithful to that call. 'Follow me.' What does that really mean? What does it mean to be a follower of Jesus? To imitate him? To walk in his steps?"

Dr. Bruce let his pen fall on the table. He could write no more. He sat staring at the papers on the table. But he didn't see the papers.

His eyes were staring through the papers, through the table, through the hotel wall, out past the darkness to a faraway place, a distant past, a screaming, hating crowd, a man, beaten

Dr. Bruce let his pen fall on the table.

and torn and bleeding, wearing a crown of thorns and carrying a great wooden cross up a hill . . .

Dr. Bruce got up and went to the window. On his face was a look of pain, of sorrow, of fear perhaps. He opened the window and stood there breathing deeply the cool night air.

The night was very still. The air was clear tonight, and the ghostly sheen of the Milky Way stretched across the velvety blackness. Ahead, the new buildings of the project at the Rectangle stood in the open field like thick, knotted warriors surrounded by the gnarled, cowering saloons and boarding houses crouching in their darkness.

Just then the clock in the First Church, several blocks away, began striking midnight. When it was finished, a voice came to Dr. Bruce, faintly, from somewhere out in the Rectangle. The singer,

He opened the window and stood there breathing deeply the cool night air.

though Dr. Bruce could never guess, was one of John Gray's converts, a man who had lived in the streets and served the god of drink and darkness, but who now sang for the God of Light. "Must Jesus bear the cross alone and all the world go free? No, there's a cross for everyone, and there's a cross for me."

Leaving the window open, Dr. Bruce crossed the room in a trance and slowly knelt by his bed. "What would Jesus do?" he whispered. "What would Jesus do?"

When he rose hours later, his hair was slicked to his forehead by sweat, and the collar of his shirt was wet with his tears.

But now a smile broke slowly over his pale, lined face. It was a smile of rest and peace and obedience. And in his eyes was a new light. He yawned and stretched and walked over to the window.

"What would Jesus do?" he whispered.

THE DAWN

The sun was just rising in the clear dawn. Its long fingers of warm, golden light gently touched the edges of the still-sleeping rows in the early-morning quiet of the Rectangle. As the sun slowly rose in the pale blue sky, its light grew and spread, reaching out over all the slowly awakening city of Raymond.

Slowly awakened city of Raymond

JOSEPH

DRAMA!
INTRIGUE!
ACTION!

AT A BOOKSTORE NEAR YOU!

ROBINSON CRUSOE

AT A BOOKSTORE NEAR YOU!

AWESOME BOOKS FOR KIDS!

The Young Reader's Christian Library
Action, Adventure, and Fun Reading!

This series for young readers ages 8 to 12 is action-packed, fast-paced, and Christ-centered! With exciting illustrations on every other page following the text, kids won't be able to put these books down! Over 100 illustrations per book. All books are paperbound. The unique size (4 3/16" x 5 3/8") makes these books easy to take anywhere!

A Great Selection to Satisfy All Kids!

Abraham Lincoln	In His Steps	Prudence of Plymouth
Ben-Hur	Jesus	Plantation
Billy Sunday	Joseph	Robinson Crusoe
Christopher Columbus	Lydia	Roger Williams
Corrie ten Boom	Miriam	Ruth
David Livingstone	Paul	Samuel Morris
Deborah	Peter	The Swiss Family
Elijah	The Pilgrim's Progress	Robinson
Esther	Pocahontas	Taming the Land
Heidi	Pollyanna	Thunder in the Valley
Hudson Taylor		Wagons West